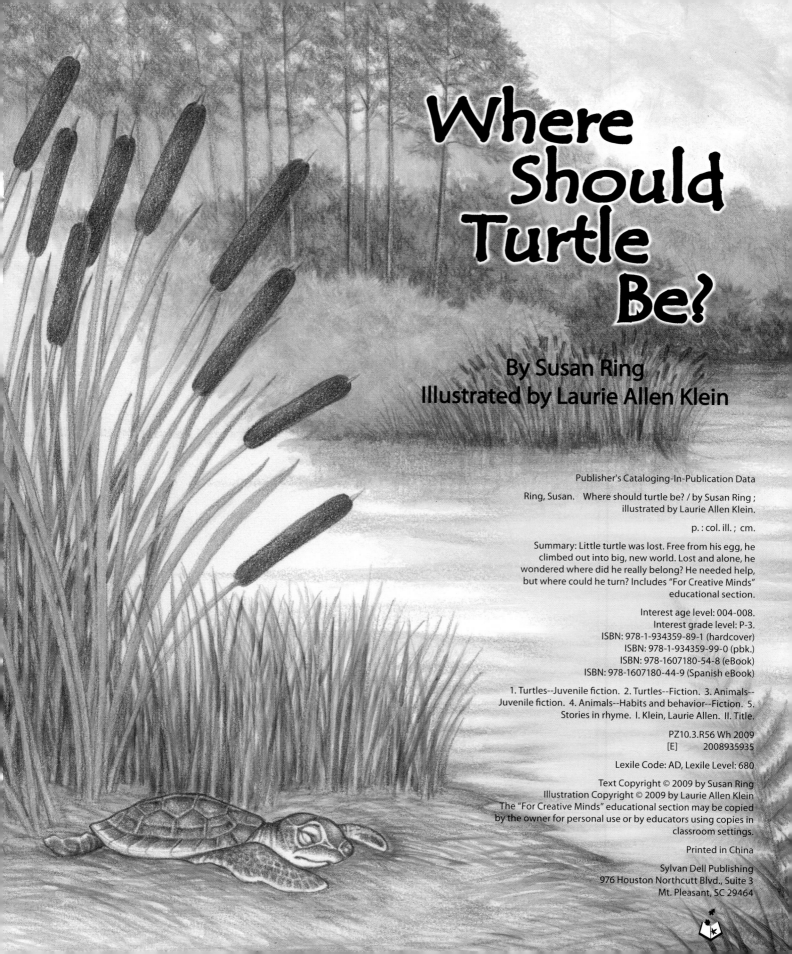

Where Should Turtle Be?

By Susan Ring
Illustrated by Laurie Allen Klein

Publisher's Cataloging-In-Publication Data

Ring, Susan.   Where should turtle be? / by Susan Ring ; illustrated by Laurie Allen Klein.

p. : col. ill. ; cm.

Summary: Little turtle was lost. Free from his egg, he climbed out into big, new world. Lost and alone, he wondered where did he really belong? He needed help, but where could he turn? Includes "For Creative Minds" educational section.

Interest age level: 004-008.
Interest grade level: P-3.
ISBN: 978-1-934359-89-1 (hardcover)
ISBN: 978-1-934359-99-0 (pbk.)
ISBN: 978-1607180-54-8 (eBook)
ISBN: 978-1607180-44-9 (Spanish eBook)

1. Turtles--Juvenile fiction. 2. Turtles--Fiction. 3. Animals--Juvenile fiction. 4. Animals--Habits and behavior--Fiction. 5. Stories in rhyme. I. Klein, Laurie Allen. II. Title.

PZ10.3.R56 Wh 2009
[E]   2008935935

Lexile Code: AD, Lexile Level: 680

Printed in China

Sylvan Dell Publishing
976 Houston Northcutt Blvd., Suite 3
Mt. Pleasant, SC 29464

To David Mahl—SR
To B & J, all my love. To my other
SW "family," thank you!—LAK

Thanks to Lou Perrotti, Conservation Coordinator, and Jim Hitchiner,
Lead Keeper, Tropics at Roger Williams Park Zoo; and to Dr. Lundie
Spence, Director, COSEE SouthEast and the South Carolina Sea Grant
Consortium, for verifying the accuracy of the information in this book.

Late one night
when you couldn't hear a sound,
there came a cracking and a popping . . .
something moving on the ground.

Inch by inch
a turtle s-l-o-w-l-y broke away
from its nest on the beach
and headed for the bay.

Guided by the lights,
he knew they were the key
to finding his new home—
wherever that should be.

But the lights weren't stars,
and the lights weren't the moon.
They were houses and cars —
and he turned too soon.

When turtle stopped to rest
by an old and crooked tree,
he said, "I think I'm lost—
this isn't where I ought to be."

Little turtle cried,
and with his tiny voice he said,
"I'm not where I should be.
I am in the woods instead."

A bear came out
when he heard the turtle's plea.
He said, "A box turtle!
That's what you could be.

"You wouldn't have to swim,
you could feast on fruit,
you could crawl around the forest,
and sleep a lot to boot."

Turtle tried it for a while,
but he couldn't stick to it.
He was not a box turtle,
and he just couldn't do it.

"No thank you," said the turtle,
"it's just not me.
I really don't think
that's what I'm supposed to be."

And so he walked on . . .

When turtle stopped to rest
by a cattail in the sun,
he said, "Where am I now?
Can you help me . . . anyone?"

Little turtle cried,
and with his tiny voice he said,
"I'm not where I should be.
I am by this pond instead."

A frog jumped down
when he heard the turtle's plea.
He said, "A painted turtle!
That's what you could be.

"You could sun on logs,
you could munch on bugs,
you could stroll around the pond,
and slurp down slugs."

Turtle tried it for a while,
but he couldn't stick to it.
He was not a painted turtle,
and he just couldn't do it.

"No thank you," said the turtle,
"it's just not me.
I really don't think
that's what I'm supposed to be."

And so he walked on . . .

Turtle was unhappy
trudging through the salty marsh.
The sun was hot, the mud was deep—
this habitat was harsh!

He pulled and yanked and flailed around
in the icky, sticky, muddy ground.
Turtle tried without much luck
but sat there stuck in gobs of muck.

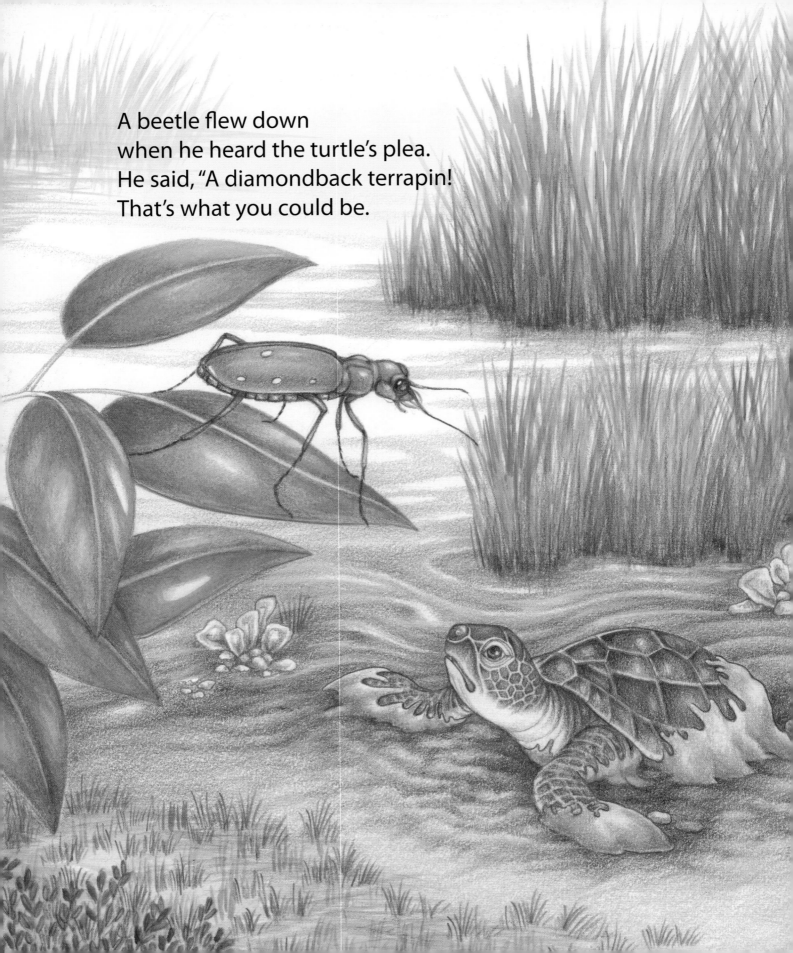

A beetle flew down
when he heard the turtle's plea.
He said, "A diamondback terrapin!
That's what you could be.

"You could crawl on the mud,
you could crunch salty snails,
you could also eat clams,
and— "

"WAIT!" the turtle shouted.
"I won't try it for a day.
I am not a terrapin,
and I must get on my way!"

Then the turtle whispered,
"You know . . . it's just not me.
I really don't think
that's what I'm supposed to be."

Then beetle tickled turtle's shell.

The turtle laughed so hard
that *POP*—he flew out from the mud—
about a mile and a yard.

Little turtle cried,
and with his tiny voice he said,
"I was looking for my home,
and, *ouch*, my head is sore instead."

A crab scurried down
when he heard the turtle's plea.
He pointed and he said, "Out there—
that's where you ought to be.

"Out there, little turtle,
it's well within your reach."
Then turtle looked around and saw
he had landed . . . on the beach.

Inch by inch
he headed out that way,
from the soft and sandy beach
to the salty, silver bay.

Then turtle slid in
and he shouted "This is me!
'Cause I'm supposed to be
a turtle in the sea."

For Creative Minds

Turtle Fun Facts

Turtles have existed for a long time. They were on the earth with the dinosaurs!

There are over 300 different types of turtles that live in habitats all over the world; including the ocean, salt marshes, wetlands, woods, grasslands, and deserts.

All turtle species lay eggs. The female turtles use their hind feet to dig a nest into which they lay their eggs. Turtles that live in water must crawl onto land to dig their nests. Sea turtles lay their nests on sandy beaches, returning to the general area where they hatched 30 to 35 years before. In the United States, these beaches are found on barrier islands in the Southeast and along the Gulf of Mexico. The hatchlings swim directly into the ocean.

Turtles don't change shells as they grow—the shell grows with them, just like our bones grow as we grow.

All turtles are reptiles that breathe air — even turtles that live in or around the water. Sea turtles must rise to the surface of the water to breathe.

Turtles are cold-blooded, which means they absorb heat from their surroundings. Many turtles may be seen basking in the sun, warming themselves. Some turtles hibernate in the winter, and sea turtles migrate to warmer waters.

Sea turtles find their way to the ocean by moving toward the brightest, most open horizon, which under natural conditions is towards the ocean. Bright lights from houses may cause the turtles to crawl the wrong way, just like the turtle in this story. Most turtles that go the wrong way are not lucky enough to survive. Some get stuck in ditches or tracks or get run over by cars.

Match the turtle adaptations

Turtle bodies are adapted to their environment. Match the description to the corresponding image. Answers are upside down on the bottom of the page.

a.

b.

1. Turtles that live in water and on land often have webbed feet for the water and claws to help them crawl on the land.

2. Sea turltes have flippers to help them swim in the ocean.

3. Painted turtles bask in the sun to get warm. You may see them on rocks or logs.

c.

4. Box turtles have a hinge so they can completely close their shells for protection!

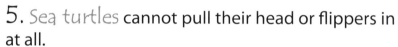

5. Sea turtles cannot pull their head or flippers in at all.

d.

6. Turtles don't have teeth like we do, but they have strong beaks that they use to crush food.

7. A turtle's shell is actually part of its skeleton. The top part, called a carapace, is really its backbone and ribs. The shape and color of the carapace is different for different types of turtles. For example, a box turtle has a high, rounded carapace—almost like a helmet, so that it can pull its head and limbs tightly inside.

e.

f.

8. The bottom part of the shell is called a plastron. Some, but not all, turtles' plastrons cover their entire body.

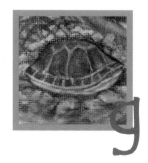

g.

h.

Match the turtle to its habitat

1.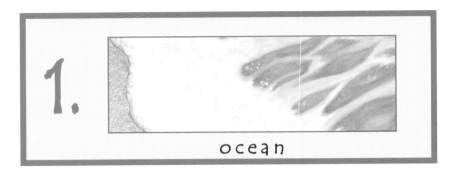
ocean

A.
box turtle

2.
woods

B.
painted turtle

3.
ponds, wetlands, and slow-moving rivers

C.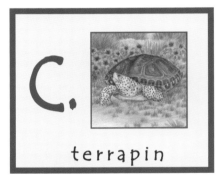
terrapin

4.
salt marsh

D.
sea turtle

answers: 1. D, 2. A, 3. B, 4. C